For Mark, for your endless love and support ~ T. C.

For Jacob ~ T. W.

tiger tales
5 River Road, Suite 128, Wilton, CT 06897
Published in the United States 2015
Originally published in Great Britain 2015
by Little Tiger Press
Text copyright © 2015 Tracey Corderoy
Illustrations copyright © 2015 Tim Warnes
Visit Tim Warnes at www.ChapmanandWarnes.com
ISBN-13: 978-1-58925-193-9
ISBN-10: 1-58925-193-8
Printed in China
LTP/1400/1133/0315

For more insight and activities, visit us at www.tigertalesbooks.com

E
65-2175

MORE!

by Tracey Corderoy

Illustrated by Tim Warnes

tiger tales

Otto was a very
BUSY rhino.

His space station was bigger than
Mom. And even bigger than Dad.
But still NOT big ENOUGH!

Otto was a very HUNGRY rhino, too.

Would you like a cupcake, Otto?

Ooo— yes, please, Grandma!

I'll just have one more . . . .

And two more . . . .

Yummy! MORE!

And Otto was a very NOISY rhino.

But even at quiet times, he ALWAYS wanted more . . . .

Whatever Otto liked,
he liked it
a LOT.

And whatever Otto did, he always did that *little* bit extra . . . .

Otto's costume was
AMAZING. Everyone
thought so . . . .

But it did make Otto too **slow** to catch up . . .

too **heavy** to bounce . . .

Maybe "more" WASN'T
always more fun.

Maybe "more" was sometimes
TOO MUCH . . . .

wheeeee!

Except, of course . . .

... when it came to having more

FRIENDS!